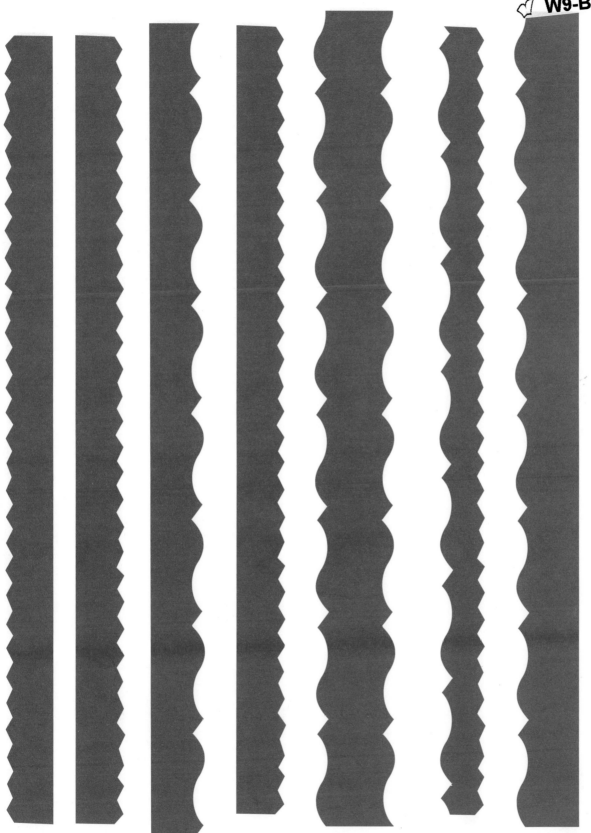

JACK AND JILL

Daniel Kirk

G. P. Putnam's Sons   New York

Library of Congress Cataloging-in-Publication Data
Kirk, Daniel. Jack and Jill / Daniel Kirk. p. cm.
Summary: In this expanded version of the familiar nursery rhyme,
Jack and his sister Jill are sent to get water from a well where they encounter a hungry crocodile.
[1. Characters in literature—Fiction. 2. Wishes—Fiction. 3. Stories in rhyme.] I. Title.
PZ8.3.K6553 Jac 2003   [E]—dc21   2002009611
ISBN 0-399-23553-1
1 3 5 7 9 10 8 6 4 2
First Impression

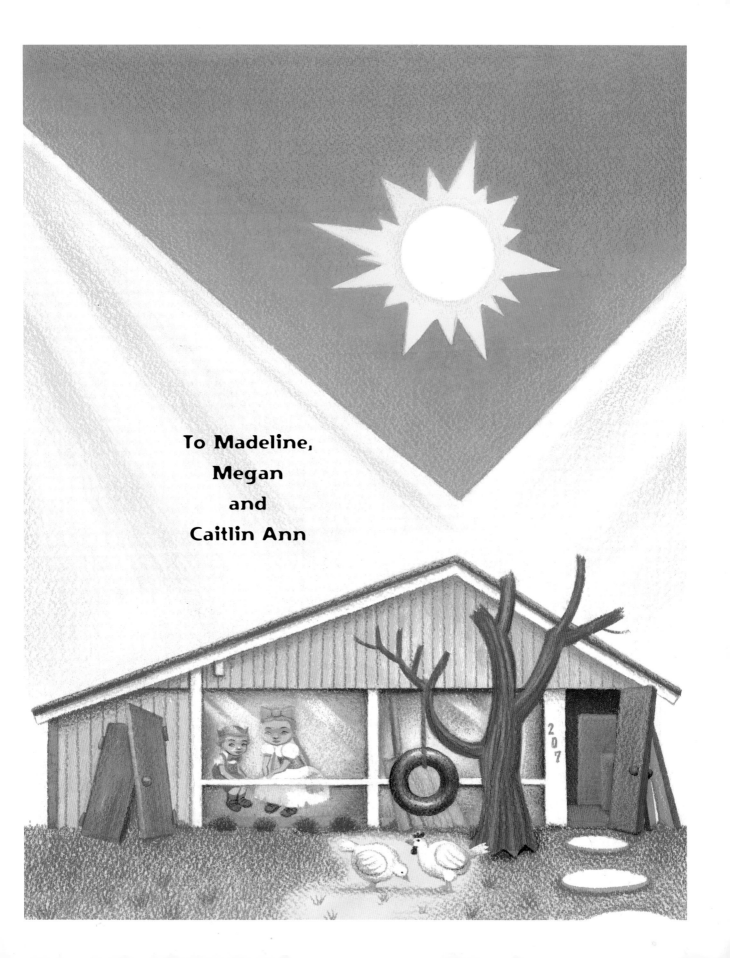

To Madeline,
Megan
and
Caitlin Ann

Jack and Jill sat on the sill
and looked out through the glass.
Their TV set was broken,
so they watched the cow eat grass.

Jill took an empty pail and put it
underneath the spout.
Jack turned the handle round and round,
but not a drop came out.

"The sink's not working, Mom," he cried.
She answered with a yell.
"Take some buckets, go outside,
get water from the well!"

Jack and Jill went up the hill;
it took them quite a while.
Jack looked in the well and screamed,
"A giant crocodile!"

The startled children jumped a mile.
"Hey, wait!" the reptile said.
But Jack fell down, and broke his crown . . .
by which I mean *his head!*

Down the rocky slope Jack rolled,
and Jill came tumbling after.
They told their mother what they'd seen.
"You kids!" She shook with laughter.

"A talking crocodile? Oh, please.
There's *no such thing*, you know.
Children, go back to the well,
as fast as you can go.

"It's true, your father vanished
when I sent him out for water. . . .
But that was quite a while ago!
Run along, my son and daughter!"

Jill hung her bucket from the hook
and gave the crank a twist.
"Stop right there—this water's mine!"
the crocodile hissed.

"The well, you see, belongs to me.
My name is Magic Sam.
I'll trade you kids some water
for a *nice, big, juicy ham!"*

"Magic Sam"—Jill trembled—
"sir, we have no meat to give.
We only need a little water
so our fish can live!"

"That breaks my heart," the croc replied,
"but children, here's the deal—
*I'll let you fill your bucket
if you bring me back a meal!"*

The children had no cash,
but with a borrowed broom and mop,
they earned some money tidying
the local butcher shop.

"Here's your ham"—the butcher smiled—
"for cleaning up the mess.
Jill, don't soil your frock—
by which I mean *your pretty dress!*"

Magic Sam was very pleased.
"You brought my favorite dish!
Since I'm feeling generous,
I'll grant you kids a wish!"

"But we need water," Jill exclaimed,
"we need it right away!"
"Make a wish," the croc replied.
"I haven't got all day!"

Magic Sam devoured the ham.
It dribbled from his snout.
"*Yuck,*" said Jill, "if only Dad
were here to help us out.

"I guess it's up to me
to make a wish, so let me think. . . .
I wish you'd send a plumber
down *to fix our broken sink!*"

"The crocodile sent me,"
said the plumber, with a cough.
He smiled and bowed, then doffed his hat—
which means he took it off.

"First," he said to Jack and Jill,
"I'll check your pipes for leaks.
With any luck, I'll have it fixed
in just a couple weeks!"

"Weeks?" cried Jill. "That's way too long.
Let's go back up the hill.
We'll beg the croc for water—
it will work, I *hope* it will!"

"Magic Sam," cried Jill,
"I'm not here to make a wish.
Won't you just be nice and
give us water for our fish?"

"What?" cried Magic Sam. "*No wish?*
I can't believe my ears!
You stubborn girl, you'll have me
shedding crocodile tears!

"Wishes are my stock in trade.
They're what I love to do.
Bring me back a side of beef—
I'll make your dream come true!"

"We're never going to earn the cash
to buy that beef," said Jack.
"If Dad were here, I bet he'd get
old Bossie from the shack!"

"We just can't trade our cow," said Jill,
"so, Brother, let me think. . . .

Perhaps that crocodile would take
a pail of *milk* to drink!"

"It's not a side of beef," said Jack,
"but milk comes from a cow,
and cows are beef—that's close enough.
Jill, you're brilliant! *Wow!*"

"*Magic Sam*," called Jill,
"we need some water right away.
We're here to make a trade.
Now I'll explain it, if I may. . . ."

But Magic Sam misunderstood.
"You kids are great," he said.
"You brought the beef, so if you want
a wish, *go right ahead!*

"Oh, *the joy!*" The big croc grinned.
"To gobble up a *cow!*"
"Darn," said Jack, "I wish that Dad
were here to help us now."

POOF! The well shot clouds of smoke.
As Jack and Jill looked on,

their long-lost dad appeared. . . .
The crocodile was gone.

"Help me up!" their father said.
"I'm grateful as can be.
The wish you asked for broke the spell
a *witch* had cast on me!

"I'd never eat you, Bossie.
Here's some grass for you to munch.
And kids, I'll fix that broken sink
right after we have lunch!

"We'll take your mother out to eat.
But first, I'd like the chance
to get these soggy breeches off—
by which I mean *my pants!*"

The happy foursome hurried home
with water for their fish;
for a well, as we all know,
is where you get your wish.